W9-CKG-883

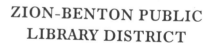

FRANCES LINCOLN CHILDREN'S BOOKS

Lord
of the Forest

Caroline Pitcher
Illustrated by Jackie Morris

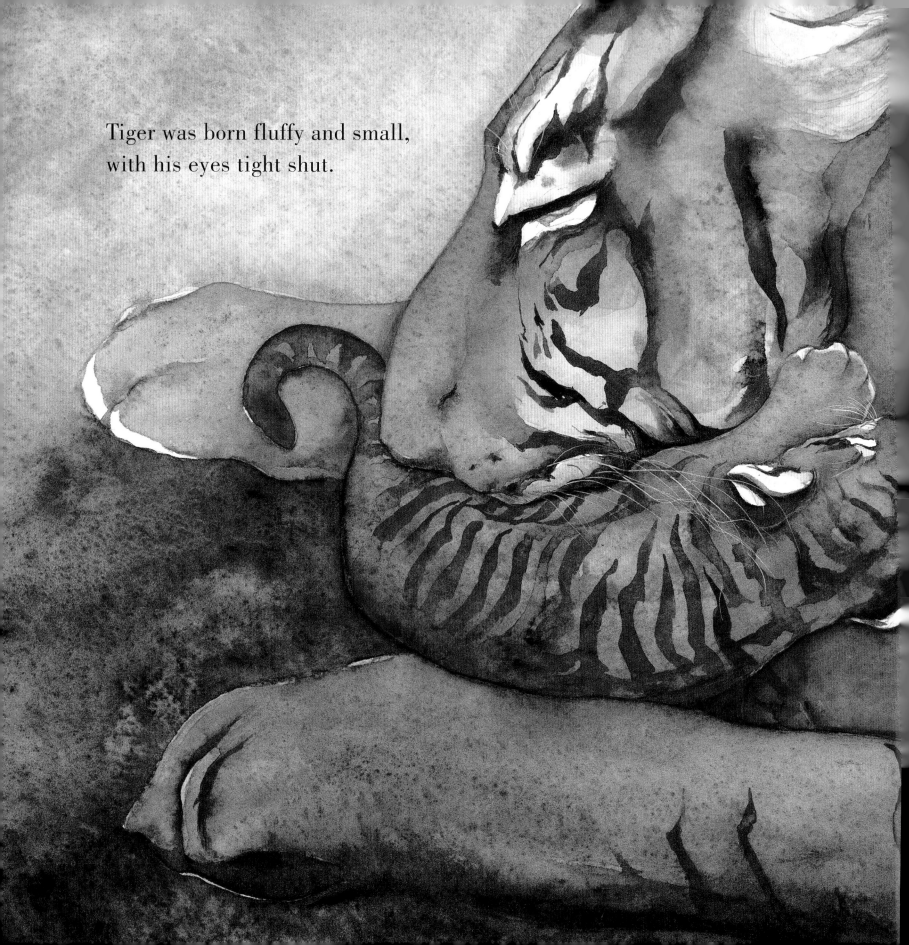

Tiger was born fluffy and small,
with his eyes tight shut.

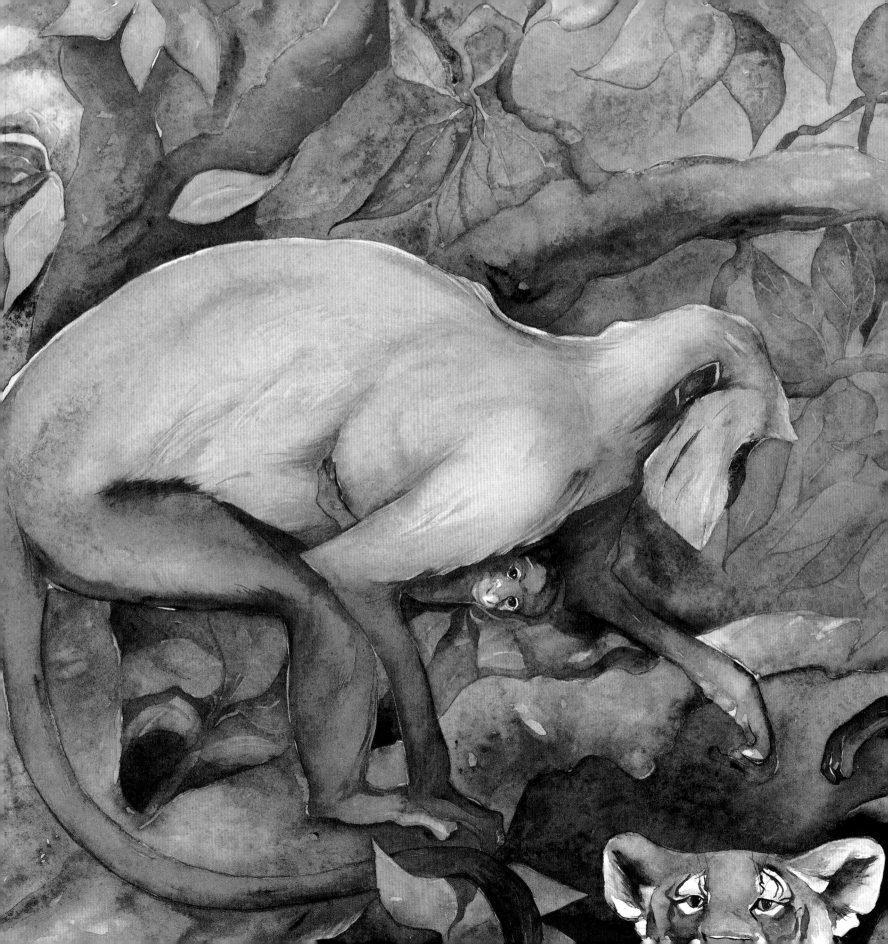

He twitched his ears and said, "I can hear the forest, the sap rising in the trees and the grass growing long after spring rain!

I hear the slither of zig-zagged snakes and the crow of Jungle Fowl when he wakes.

I hear Monkey whooping to his tribe and the shudder of the branch as he jumps.

I can even hear the curling of Chameleon's tongue and the gulp of little Gekko in the green."

His mother said, "When you don't hear the forest, when silence simmers in the trees, then, my son, be ready.

The Lord of the Forest is on his way!"

Tiger played and fought with his brothers. He swam in the cool water.

He told his mother, "I can hear the creep of crabs from the pool and the flip of fish as they leap in the cool, the croak and splash of jumping frogs and the slither of Water-snake down from the logs."

His mother said, "When you don't hear them, when silence burns and time stands still, then, my son, be ready.

The Lord of the Forest is here!"

Tiger prowled in the mornings when the sun streamed through the mist.

He stalked in the evenings on powerful paws with scimitar claws, and his eyes were worlds of wildness.

When Tiger was grown,
he walked alone.
His shoulder-blades slid
under his golden skin,
rippling through the forest.
He was grass-shadowed and
eye-dazzle bright, a stealthy
cat alone in the night, solitary
cat, with mirrors in his eyes.

Tiger lived his days by lakes
and rocky ridges. He heard
Eagle soaring in the sky and
Ant scuttling down on the earth.

He said, "I am still listening
for that silence, still waiting
for the Lord of the Forest.

Who is the Lord of the Forest?"

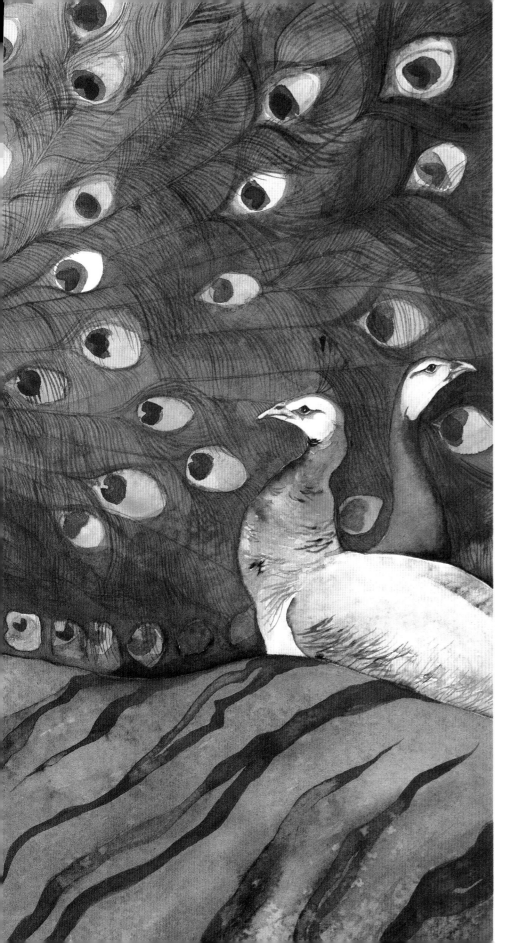

"It's me!" screeched Peacock,
strutting with his hens. "I am
lordly, Tiger! Can't you see?
My tail is magnificent!
My feathers are holy.
I kill snakes with my claws!"

Peacock rattled his quills.
His tail with its thousand
feather eyes spangled in
the sun around his tiny head.

Tiger said, "Your tail
is beautiful, Peacock,
but the Lord of the Forest
does not shriek and screech.

Who is the Lord of the Forest?"

"It's me!" roared Rhino, blundering through the trees. "Look at my suit of armour! Look at my deadly horn!"

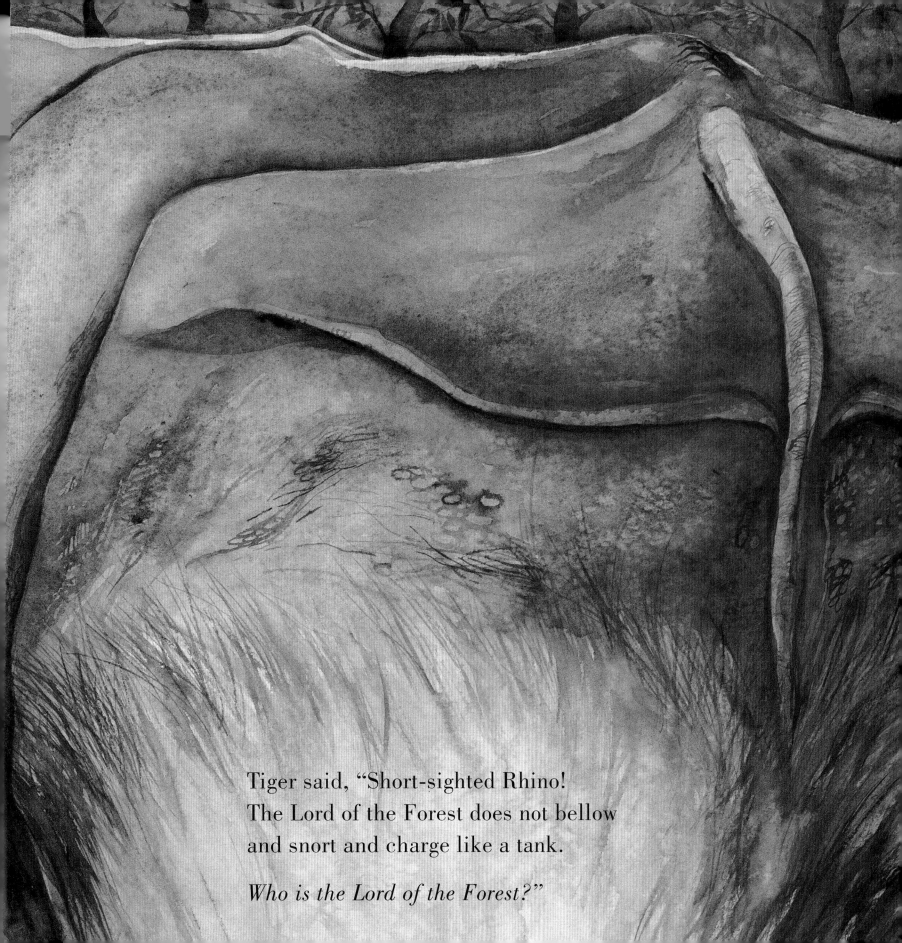

Tiger said, "Short-sighted Rhino!
The Lord of the Forest does not bellow
and snort and charge like a tank.

Who is the Lord of the Forest?"

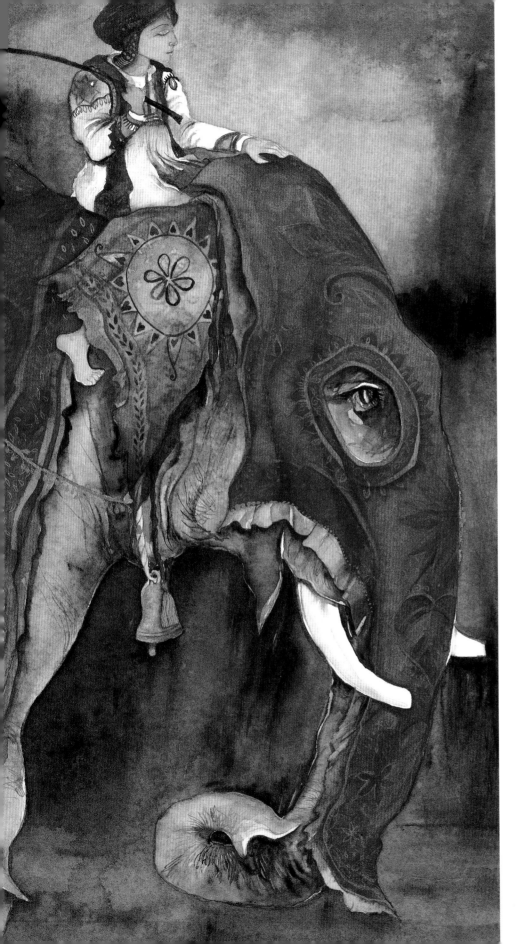

"It's me, of course," trumpeted Elephant, swaying like a ship, his little mahout perched high on his back. "See my tusks gleam! Hear my bells ring!"

Peacock dashed away, shrieking like a cat. Rhino bellowed — and charged into a tree. Elephant stopped short and roared.

"The Lord of the Forest cannot be so noisy," said Tiger. "The Lord of the Forest would never carry people on his back.

Who is the Lord of the Forest?"

Proud Tiger saw a tigress slipping golden
through the grass. He watched the white tips
of her ears and her umbrella-hook tail
held high. Her sides were patterned black,
ferns against the sun.

Tiger and his tigress had cubs, fluffy and small,
with their eyes tight shut. Tiger loved them so!
He licked their faces with his great rough tongue,
nuzzling and purring while he pinned them down.

In the midday heat, Tiger lounged under the fragrant mowa tree, as comfortable as only a cat can be.

He prowled up to his rocky ridge and stood between heaven and earth.
He stretched his jaws wide and roared, "TIGER!"
He stood there still as a statue, and heard… nothing!
Silence simmered in the trees.
Fear scorched the grass.

"Where are you, Lord of the Forest?" he roared.
"Show yourself!"

And then the tigress called him from the pool…

"He's here," she purred.
"Look in the water.

The Lord of the Forest is – you!"

For Joy – C.P.

*For Thomas and Hannah, in the hope that when
your children's children read this book, there will still
be tigers roaming the wild places of the world – J.M.*

Lord of the Forest copyright © Frances Lincoln Limited 2004
Text copyright © Caroline Pitcher 2004
Illustrations copyright © Jackie Morris 2004

First published in Great Britain in 2004 by Frances Lincoln Children's Books,
4 Torriano Mews, Torriano Avenue, London NW5 2RZ
www.franceslincoln.com

Distributed in the USA by Publishers Group West

British Library Cataloguing in Publication Data available on request

ISBN 1-84507-058-5

Set in Bodoni

Printed in Singapore
9 8 7 6 5 4 3 2 1

**Visit the Lord of the Forest website
at www.lordoftheforest.co.uk
and Caroline Pitcher's website
at www.carolinepitcher.co.uk**